THREE-LEGGED HERO

A Military Dog Story

by Spencer Brinker

illustrated by Robin Lawrie

BEARPORT PUBLISHING

New York, New York

Credits

Cover photo, © Eric Isselée/Fotolia.

Publisher: Kenn Goin
Editor: Jessica Rudolph
Creative Director: Spencer Brinker

Library of Congress Cataloging-in-Publication Data in process at time of publication (2017)
Library of Congress Control Number: 2016050048
ISBN-13: 978-1-68402-014-0

For more information, write to Bearport Publishing Company, Inc., 45 West 21st Street, Suite 3B, New York, New York 10010. Printed in the United States of America.

10 9 8 7 6 5 4 3 2 1

CONTENTS

WELCOME TO **HOUND TOWN**

A Doggone Nice Place to Live!

Population:
25,000 people
20,000 dogs

CHAPTER 1

Cali's Dog-Walking Service

An energetic white and brown dog raced around eleven-year-old Cali, barking happily. "Soon, Trixie, relax!" said Cali.

Dad was folding laundry into neat piles. As Cali shoved a stack of flyers into her backpack, one of the flyers fell out and landed near Dad's feet. He picked it up and read aloud: "'Cali's Dog-Walking Service. Professional Care. Reasonable Rates.' Looks good, sweetheart. I'd trust you with my dog. In fact, I already *do* trust you with my dog. Isn't that right, girl?" Dad reached down and scratched Trixie behind her floppy ears. The little dog gave two loud, excited barks.

"*Our* dog, Dad!" said Cali. "And Trixie's easy—she practically walks me." Cali threw a roll of tape into her backpack. "But I'm just not sure how my two new dog **clients** are going to behave. Have you seen Trixie's leash?" she asked.

"It's right there," said Dad. He pointed to the leash hanging over the door handle. "Oh, and Cal, don't forget these," he said, handing

Cali several plastic bags tied into a bunch. "With your new business, you have to be sure to pick up and throw away any, um . . . *business* . . . that the dogs might leave on the sidewalk."

"Oh, right. Thanks!" said Cali. She quickly shoved the bags into her backpack. After clipping Trixie's leash to her collar, Cali gave Dad a quick kiss on the cheek and headed out the door.

When Cali and Trixie arrived at the house of a neighbor named Mr. London, Cali rang the bell. The door opened and next to Mr. London was a large, friendly looking Dalmatian. Trixie and the spotted dog started sniffing one another. "Hi there," said Mr. London. "Duke's all ready. He likes to explore the neighborhood a bit. That's okay, isn't it?" he asked.

Cali looked a bit unsure. "Oh, yes. That's fine," she said quickly. "Um, what do you mean by *explore*?"

"Oh, Duke just likes to have fun," he said. "Okay, see you later," Mr. London said as he handed the leash to Cali and closed the door.

Not quite sure what to think, Cali led Duke and Trixie to the sidewalk and headed toward a yellow house. When Duke stepped out ahead of Trixie, she barked loudly at him. Duke stopped and looked at her curiously. Cali smiled.

The blue door to the yellow house opened just as Cali arrived, and out stepped an elderly woman in a long flowing bathrobe trimmed with fluffy pink feathers. In her arms was a small Chihuahua. "Yoo-hoo! Hello!" the woman said in a loud, musical voice.

"Hi, Mrs. Baker," said Cali. She held tightly on to Duke's and Trixie's leashes as Mrs. Baker carefully set down her small dog.

"Cali! Mr. Chi-chi is absolutely ready for his walk. He's been so excited all morning. But you must promise to have him back within the hour—it's our grooming day you see, and we can't miss that! Oh, a Dalmatian. How *is* your father, dear?" Mrs. Baker said all of this very quickly.

"My dad is fine, thanks," said Cali. "And we won't be long."

"Oh, good," said Mrs. Baker. "Hold the leash tightly. Mr. Chi-chi can be a handful!"

Cali took the leash from Mrs. Baker and looked down at the shivering dog. "I think we'll be fine," said Cali.

When Mrs. Baker went back into her house, Cali slipped her backpack off and took out the roll of tape and stack of flyers.

"Come on, guys," Cali said as she gently pulled on the leashes. "Let's put up some flyers." Duke took two large steps forward before Trixie moved in front of him. Mr. Chi-chi followed behind the other two dogs, taking small **tentative** steps.

After walking for a few minutes, Cali stopped at a lamppost, and the dogs waited patiently while she taped a flyer to it. "There," said Cali, satisfied. Then she led the dogs around a corner down a short

cul-de-sac. Cali spotted another lamppost near a brown house with a big garden beside it. She headed toward the house with the dogs.

As they neared the lamppost, Duke spotted a butterfly fluttering above the flowers in the garden. Suddenly, he leaped toward the insect. Cali fell and was dragged several feet. She used all her strength just to keep hold of the three leashes. Her flyers went everywhere.

"Do you need some help, honey?" called a clear voice. Cali looked up and saw a woman with a slight limp walking across the lawn. Next to her was a German shepherd that seemed to be hopping. Cali realized the dog was missing one of its front legs.

9

CHAPTER 2

Thunder

"Let me give you a hand," said the woman as she helped Cali up. Duke had already forgotten the butterfly. He and Trixie were happily sniffing the German shepherd, who was equally happy to sniff them in return. Mr. Chi-chi was nervously watching everyone.

"Thank you. Duke ran after a butterfly," Cali explained, feeling embarrassed.

"Oh, I get it, hon," said the woman kindly. She knelt down to help gather the flyers. "Dogs can be **mischievous**. There's a pound of trouble for a pound of hound. That's what my grandma used to say. By the way, I'm Sarah," she said, holding out her hand.

Cali smiled and shook Sarah's hand. "My name's Cali. The dogs aren't all mine. Just Trixie here."

"Yes, I see," said Sarah, reading one of the flyers. "Good for you, having your own business. At your age, I was getting into all sorts of trouble. That's probably why I eventually joined the military—to straighten myself out a bit."

"You're a soldier?" Cali asked.

"I used to be in the Marines," said Sarah. "Marine Corporal Suarez, stationed in Afghanistan," she said, giving a playful **salute**. "And

this amazing guy was *also* a soldier—his name is Thunder," she said, scratching the German shepherd behind his ears. Sarah suddenly sneezed. "Excuse me!" she said. "**Allergy** season has started."

"Bless you!" said Cali. "Umm . . . your dog was a *soldier*?"

After hearing his name, Thunder did a short hop and skip and sat down next to Sarah.

"Yes, Thunder was a soldier too," Sarah said. "He was a weapons- and **bomb**-detection dog. . . . You know, Thunder could use a good dog walker. And you're looking for new clients. What do you think?"

Cali looked doubtfully at Thunder's front leg. "Well, sure," she said. "But can he . . . I mean, does he walk okay?"

Sarah smiled. "Both Thunder and I have to work a little harder to get around these days. But we manage just fine. Watch this, hon." Sarah picked up a nearby stick and showed it to Thunder. "Hey, Thunder! Wanna fetch?"

Thunder stood up quickly and gave one quick, eager bark. "Ready, boy? *Go!*" Sarah said as she threw the stick high in the air.

Thunder burst forward in a speeding hop-skip across the lawn. Then he leaped into the air, caught the stick in his mouth, and landed on the soft grass. He proudly made his way back to Sarah while Duke and Trixie barked excitedly.

Cali's mouth hung open. "*Wow!*" she said. "That was awesome! Trixie could never do that!"

Sarah sneezed into her tissue three times quickly. "I'm sorry," she said. "But I've got to get inside. My allergies are getting bad. So, can Thunder join you for a walk tomorrow?"

"Of course he can!" said Cali. She made arrangements to pick up Thunder the next day. On her way home, Cali thought about how she couldn't wait to tell her dad all about meeting *two* soldiers.

CHAPTER 3

The Walk

The next day, Cali arrived at Sarah's house with the three dogs, walked up to the front porch, and knocked on the door. Sarah opened the door and smiled. "Hey, Cali," she said. "How are you doing, hon?" Thunder went over to the other dogs and wagged his tail playfully.

"Hey," said Cali. "Hi, Thunder. We're all ready."

"Good!" said Sarah. "Let me grab Thunder's leash." Sarah disappeared into the house. Just inside the door, Cali saw a framed photo on the wall that showed Sarah dressed in **fatigues**. She was standing in what looked like a dusty military camp. Next to Sarah was Thunder—standing proudly for the camera. He had all four legs.

"Okay, all set," said Sarah as she walked up with Thunder's leash in her hand. She attached one end of the leash to Thunder's collar and gave the other end of it to Cali.

"Thanks," said Cali. "I guess we're ready." She looked nervously down at Thunder, Duke, Trixie, and Mr. Chi-chi. This was the first time she'd be walking four dogs by herself.

"You'll be fine," said Sarah. "Thunder's a sweetheart."

Cali said good-bye and headed to the sidewalk.

At first, walking all four dogs was a bit of a challenge. Duke wandered from side to side. *Probably looking for butterflies!* Cali thought. Trixie walked confidently in front, but would turn around and bark whenever Duke wandered too far. Mr. Chi-chi kept looking anxiously at the German shepherd. Only Thunder, despite his hop-skip way of moving, appeared calm.

Cali was impressed by just how easy it was to walk Thunder. When she pulled gently on the leashes and said "Stop" at street corners, Thunder stopped and waited patiently. He wouldn't pull ahead or move too slowly. When the dogs found an old sock on the sidewalk, Thunder obeyed when Cali gave the **command**, "Leave it!"

On their way back, Cali and the dogs passed a house with a row of low bushes. Suddenly, Cali heard a loud *Hissssssss*! She turned around and saw a large orange cat with an arched back. It was hissing angrily at Mr. Chi-chi. The cat, which was about twice the size of the frightened Chihuahua, looked as if it might swipe at the dog with its sharp claws.

Just as Cali began to pull back on Mr. Chi-chi's leash, Thunder leaped forward and landed between the hissing cat and the shaking Chihuahua. He stood firmly facing the cat and gave a loud, forceful *Woof!* The terrified cat turned quickly and disappeared into the bushes. Thunder immediately relaxed and sat down.

Cali held tightly to Duke's and Trixie's leashes—both dogs seemed determined to chase after the cat. When the two dogs finally calmed down, Cali bent down to pet the trembling Mr. Chi-chi.

"It's okay now," she said. "Let's get you home."

When the group got to Mr. Chi-chi's house, Mrs. Baker opened the door wearing a flowery apron. "You're back Chi-chi-kins! How are you, darling?" she said.

Cali explained what happened with the cat, and how Thunder had defended Mr. Chi-chi. Mrs. Baker looked shocked. She picked her dog up and hugged him tightly, and then seemed to notice Thunder for the first time. "What's wrong with his leg?" she asked.

"Oh, Thunder was a soldier in Afghanistan!" said Cali, happy to share this remarkable information.

"But what on earth happened to him, dear? Oh no—never mind! I don't want to know," she said, looking at Mr. Chi-chi as if something might happen to his leg too. "I must be going. Mr. Chi-chi needs to rest after his scary encounter! Good-bye, dear," said Mrs. Baker, and she closed her door.

After dropping Duke off at Mr. London's house, Cali led Thunder and Trixie back to Sarah's house. When Sarah came outside to greet them, Thunder jumped up on her affectionately, his tail wagging wildly. "Hey, Thunder, how was your walk?" asked Sarah.

Cali told Sarah how well behaved Thunder had been, and how he had protected the Chihuahua from the cat. "He was very brave. The cat could have done some damage with those sharp claws," Cali said.

"That doesn't surprise me," said Sarah. "Thunder is fearless." Thunder rolled over on his back, and Sarah knelt down to rub his

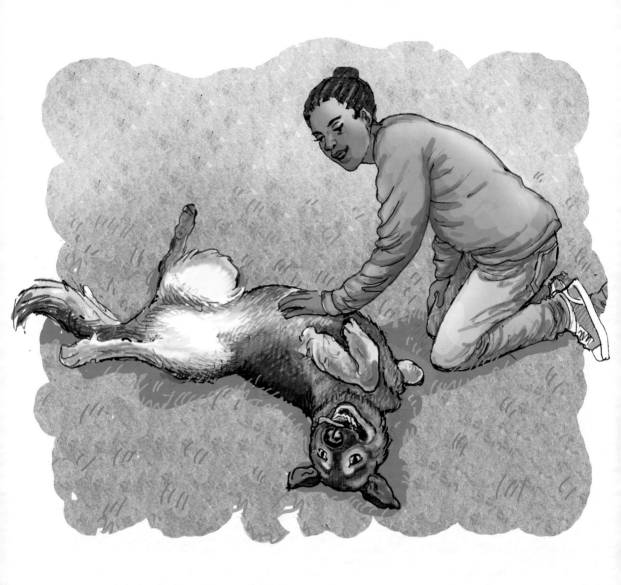

tummy. Cali could see the bump where Thunder's leg used to be.

"Um, how did that happen?" asked Cali. "I mean, how did Thunder lose his leg?"

Sarah looked up. "It was from a bomb that exploded in Afghanistan," she said. "Thunder risked his life to save me."

CHAPTER 4

A Military Dog's Story

Cali was nearly speechless. "A bomb?" she said as she stared down at Thunder, who was still rolling on his back, hoping Sarah would rub his belly a bit more.

"Yes," said Sarah. "It's quite a story. Why don't you come on in, have some lemonade, and I'll tell you about it. From inside, my allergies won't bother me so much."

Cali and Trixie followed Sarah and Thunder into the house. Trixie sniffed around the room for a minute and then lay down on the floor next to Thunder. Sarah invited Cali to sit at the kitchen table.

"I've never heard of a dog soldier before. Are there others besides Thunder?" asked Cali.

"Oh, yes, there are lots of dogs working in the military," said Sarah. "More than two thousand in total, with about seven hundred of those stationed overseas." Sarah handed Cali a glass of lemonade.

"Thanks," said Cali. "Wow, I had no idea."

"Dogs have actually been part of military work for thousands of years," said Sarah. "And they make incredible soldiers."

Sarah brought over a plate of cookies and set them on the table. Then she continued, "Thunder's military training started when he was

just a puppy. Later, he was sent over to Afghanistan to help with the war, and that's when I met him. I had arrived with my Marine unit about a month beforehand and was assigned to be one of Thunder's **handlers**. That's what they call soldiers who work with a **service dog**."

"Everyone on the **base** loved Thunder," said Sarah. She had a look in her eyes as if she was remembering a happy dream. "He learned his job quickly and always worked hard."

"Our Marine unit was responsible for entering buildings and **compounds** to make sure there were no hidden bombs that could harm our troops. It was very dangerous work," said Sarah. She paused to take a sip of lemonade.

"You said that Thunder could find bombs or weapons?" asked Cali. "How?"

"With his nose, hon," said Sarah. "I'm sure you know that a dog has an amazing sense of smell. Thunder was trained to find bombs and weapons by scent. He could detect the tiniest traces of materials that are used to make weapons."

Sarah went on. "When we arrived at a building that needed to be checked, the other Marines and I would slowly approach the entrance, letting Thunder lead the way. He carefully smelled the ground and the edges of the walls. We trusted his senses to safely guide us."

Cali was fascinated. "How would you know if he found something?" she asked.

"He would stop and stare at the place where his nose told him a weapon or bomb was hidden and he would bark quietly," Sarah said. "Then a special team wearing protective equipment would come in to uncover and **deactivate** the explosive."

"One day, we were sent out to investigate a building," Sarah said. "Suddenly our unit was attacked—there was gunfire all around us.

We were forced to take cover inside a building that we hadn't yet checked."

"When we stepped into the building," said Sarah, "there was a flash of blinding light and a huge *BOOM!* At first I was **dazed**. Then I tried to get up, but I couldn't move. I had **shrapnel** in my leg from the bomb, and it was bleeding badly. I could barely see because there was black smoke everywhere."

"Then I started to hear Thunder barking near me," said Sarah. "He was trying to tell the other members of my team where I was. He kept barking, even with all the noise, smoke, and confusion. Eventually, my team found me and took me to the hospital. The doctors said that if Thunder hadn't been there, I might have bled to death."

Cali swallowed hard. "Whoa, that's amazing. So, Thunder was hurt in that explosion, too?"

"Yes," said Sarah. "I didn't know it at the time, but his leg was hurt even worse than mine. But he still saved me. He's a real hero."

"They sent me home to recover," explained Sarah, "but I couldn't forget Thunder. I made a ton of phone calls and sent out a bunch of emails to find him. Finally, I learned that Thunder had survived. His leg had been **amputated**, and he was sent back to the United States to recover, too. So, I did what I needed to do to **adopt** him. And, well, here we are. He's my best friend in the world," she said, smiling.

CHAPTER 5

Still a Hero

"Dad, my business is going under!" said Cali. She knelt down to put a leash on Trixie. "Duke is going on vacation with Mr. London, and Mrs. Baker wants Mr. Chi-chi to take a break from walks because the weather has cooled down a bit," said Cali, rolling her eyes.

Trixie started to drag Cali out the door. "Business will pick up, sweetheart," Dad called after her. "Don't worry!"

On her way to Sarah's house, Cali thought about the past seven days—one full week with her own dog-walking service. Duke had tried to chase insects a few times, and Mr. Chi-chi was still a little jittery. Cali thought, *Maybe today will be more relaxing with only Trixie and Thunder to worry about.*

When Cali knocked on Sarah's door, she heard a loud sneeze as soon as it opened. "Sorry!" said Sarah. "These allergies have gotten worse." Her eyes looked red and puffy.

Thunder hopped over to Trixie excitedly. "Hi, Thunder," said Cali. "It's just us today, Sarah. The others couldn't make it. I'm sorry you don't feel well."

Sarah sneezed again into a tissue. "Thanks, hon," she said. "Listen, is there any chance you could take Thunder on a longer walk today? I've taken some new allergy medicine, I'm making a cup of tea, and I just want to rest for a while."

"Oh, no problem," said Cali. "We can do the short loop, then pass by here and head over to the park. That's a nice long walk, and it should be fun." Cali said good-bye and headed off with the dogs.

About an hour after leaving, Cali and the dogs looped back and passed by Sarah's house. As the group walked by the house, Thunder suddenly stopped. "What's the matter, boy?" Cali said.

Thunder barked, then he pulled on the leash toward Sarah's door. Cali held tightly. "Come on, Thunder. You're not going home yet. We're going to the park first," she said.

Just then, Thunder leaped and pulled the leash from Cali's hand. He dashed toward the front door.

"Thunder, stop!" cried Cali. She ran after the German shepherd. Trixie followed her, barking noisily at her side.

Thunder bounded up the porch and barked at the door. *Woof! Woof!* Cali began to get worried. She knocked on the door. "Sarah?" she said loudly. "Hello?"

Thunder hop-skipped over to a nearby window. He began barking again. *Woof! Woof!*

Cali tried to look into the window, but the curtains were drawn. She banged hard on the glass. "Sarah! Are you there?" she yelled. Finally, Sarah's sleepy face appeared at the window.

"Sarah!" shouted Cali. "Something's wrong with Thunder."

Sarah had a worried expression on her face. She motioned to the front door then disappeared behind the curtains. After a few seconds, the door opened. Sarah limped out quickly, leading Cali and the dogs away from the house.

"It was the gas stove," Sarah said breathlessly. "I forgot to turn it off, and then I fell asleep because of the medicine. I think a breeze blew out the flame on the stove. Thunder must have smelled the gas. If he hadn't woken me . . . He saved my life . . . again!"

Cali looked down at Thunder, who was now sitting calmly next to Sarah. "He's unbelievable," said Cali. "It looks like Thunder is *still* a hero!"

Three-Legged Hero
A Military Dog Story

1. What do you think Cali is feeling when she begins the first day of her new dog-walking business?

2. What does Sarah do to show Cali that Thunder won't have any problems going on a walk?

3. What is happening in this scene?

4. What happened in Afghanistan that made Sarah want to adopt Thunder?

5. At the end of the story, why does Cali say that Thunder is still a hero?

GLOSSARY

adopt (uh-DAHPT) to take in as part of a family

allergy (AL-ur-jee) a reaction of the body to dust, pollen, or animals, causing sneezing, itchy eyes, or other symptoms

amputated (AM-pyoo-*tay*-tid) cut off from the body because of an injury or infection

base (BAYSS) a place from which military operations are controlled

bomb (BAHM) a container filled with explosives

clients (KLYE-uhnts) people who use professional services

command (kuh-MAND) an order given to a person or animal

compounds (KAHM-poundz) fenced-in or walled-in areas with buildings inside

cul-de-sac (KUHL-duh-*sak*) a road that is closed at one end

dazed (DAYZD) stunned; unable to think clearly

deactivate (dee-AK-tuh-vayt) to make inactive or not operational

fatigues (fuh-TEEGZ) military uniform with a camouflage pattern

handlers (HAND-lurz) people who help train or manage working dogs

mischievous (MISS-chuh-vuhss) able to cause trouble, often through playful behavior

salute (suh-LOOT) a gesture of raising the right hand to the forehead as a sign of respect; used in the military

service dog (SUR-viss DAWG) a dog trained to do special tasks for people

shrapnel (SHRAP-nuhl) small metal pieces from an exploded bomb

tentative (TEN-tuh-tiv) hesitant or unsure

About the Author

Spencer Brinker lives and works in New York City. A designer by profession, he's enjoyed his recent foray into writing, and stories about animals are especially satisfying. While Spencer doesn't own a dog, he enjoys being in a city where hundreds of thousands of canines walk on the sidewalks and play in the parks. At home, his twin daughters have two lovable guinea pigs, Skittles and Strawberry, who add a playful element to his family life.

About the Illustrator

Robin Lawrie, a Scotsman who grew up in Vancouver, Canada, started his career as an author and illustrator in London. He now lives in an old barn in England, which has a bat sanctuary in the attic. He has illustrated almost 300 children's books, and he has written 21, mostly about one of his hobbies—downhill mountain biking. He has also adapted *The Lion, the Witch and the Wardrobe* and *The Magician's Nephew* into graphic novels.